I0650006

Thank you to Buddy the bear for sharing his amazing adventures, and a special thank you to all his family and friends that support his journeys.

BUDDY THE BEAR

Story by Victoria Allen

Illustrations By Ovidiu Toma

As the sun went down and the moon appeared, Buddy did not fear the dark because he has a special Goodnight Box. It is filled with goodies that help him sleep.

Buddy pulled out his fuzzy pajamas that keep him warm at night and he put them on.

Buddy put up his stars that glow and twinkle all through the night.

Then Buddy turned on his rocket night light
that shines to help him see in the dark.

But when Buddy reached into the Goodnight Box for his favorite goodie of all, it was not there! "Oh no! Where's my blanket?!" he cried.

Buddy felt that he could not sleep without his bedtime blanket! He looked for it everywhere in his room, but could not find it there.

Finally, Buddy looked out his window and he saw it! The blanket was up in the sky with all of the stars.

He had to go get it, but he knew he must be back in time for his bedtime story.

Buddy hopped on his rocket and prepared for take-off.

"3...2...1... Blast Off!" yelled Buddy.

His rocket zoomed into the stars. The stars smiled at him as he whizzed by. He saw his blanket in the distance. He got closer and closer...

Oh no! There's a problem.
The blanket is stuck on a star!

Buddy pulled and pulled and pulled.

Finally, with one last tug, he got it loose!

"I must get back for my bedtime story!" Buddy worried. But while he was flying around the sky, Buddy had gotten lost.

Buddy began to cry. "Why are you crying, Buddy?" asked the stars.
"I c-c-can't remember how to get home!" he sobbed.

"We will help you, Buddy." The stars promised.

Soon the stars all lined up to make a brightly shining path to show him the way back home. "Thank you, stars!" shouted Buddy.

Buddy launched his rocket boosters and waved goodnight to the stars. He sped back home holding tightly to his bedtime blanket.

Buddy made it home - just in time!

Holding his special blanket, he hopped in bed.

Soon, the door opened and in came Big Bear to read a bedtime story - Buddy's favorite part of the night.

Buddy snuggled up with Big Bear to listen to his story as the stars twinkled "goodnight" in the sky.

CPSIA information can be obtained at www.ICGtesting.com
Printed in the USA
BVIW12n1305221117
500935BV00003B/1

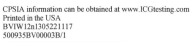